KU-634-741

This book belongs to:

....

7 8 4 3 6 2

9 2 6 9 7 5

5 7 5 8 9 3

1 10 2 1 4

8 4 5 3 7

5 7 9 4 5 10

HODDER CHILDREN'S BOOKS
First published in Great Britain in 2012 by Hodder Children's Books
This paperback edition published in 2017 by Hodder and Stoughton

A CIP catalogue record for this book is available from the British Library.

ISBN: 978 1 444 90847 3

10 9 8 7 6 5 4 3 2 1

Printed and bound in China

FSC
www.fsc.org
MIX
Paper from
responsible sources
FSC® C104740

Hodder Children's Books
An imprint of Hachette Children's Group
Part of Hodder and Stoughton
Carmelite House
50 Victoria Embankment
London EC4Y 0DZ

An Hachette UK Company
www.hachette.co.uk

www.hachettechildrens.co.uk

1, 2, 3, SPLOSH!

DAVID MELLING

Hodder
Children's
Books

ONE fluffy duck goes waddling one day.

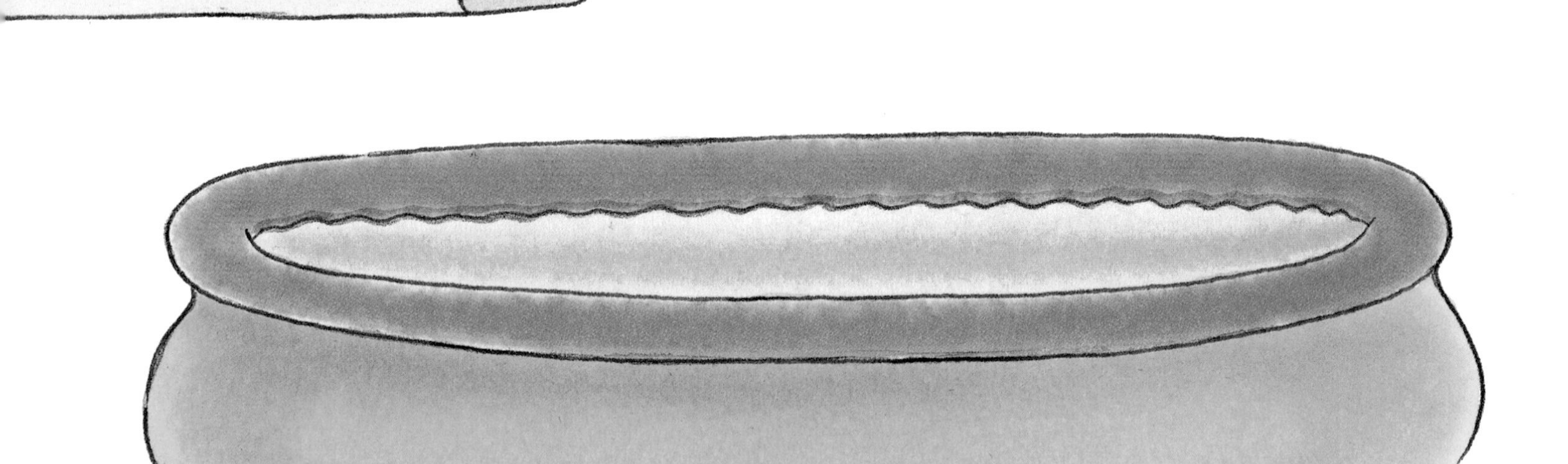

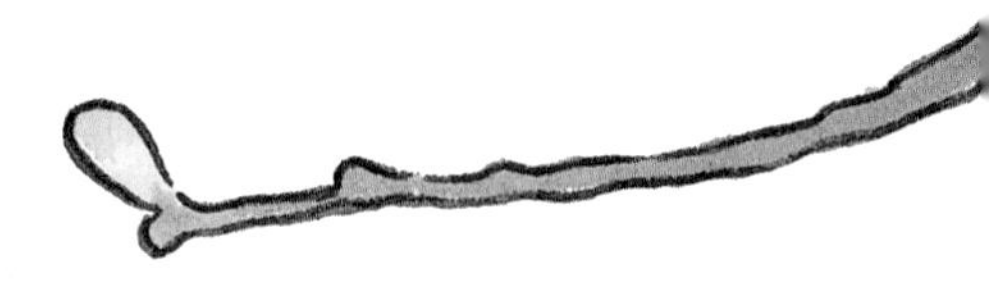

TWO fluffy ducks have found
a place to play!

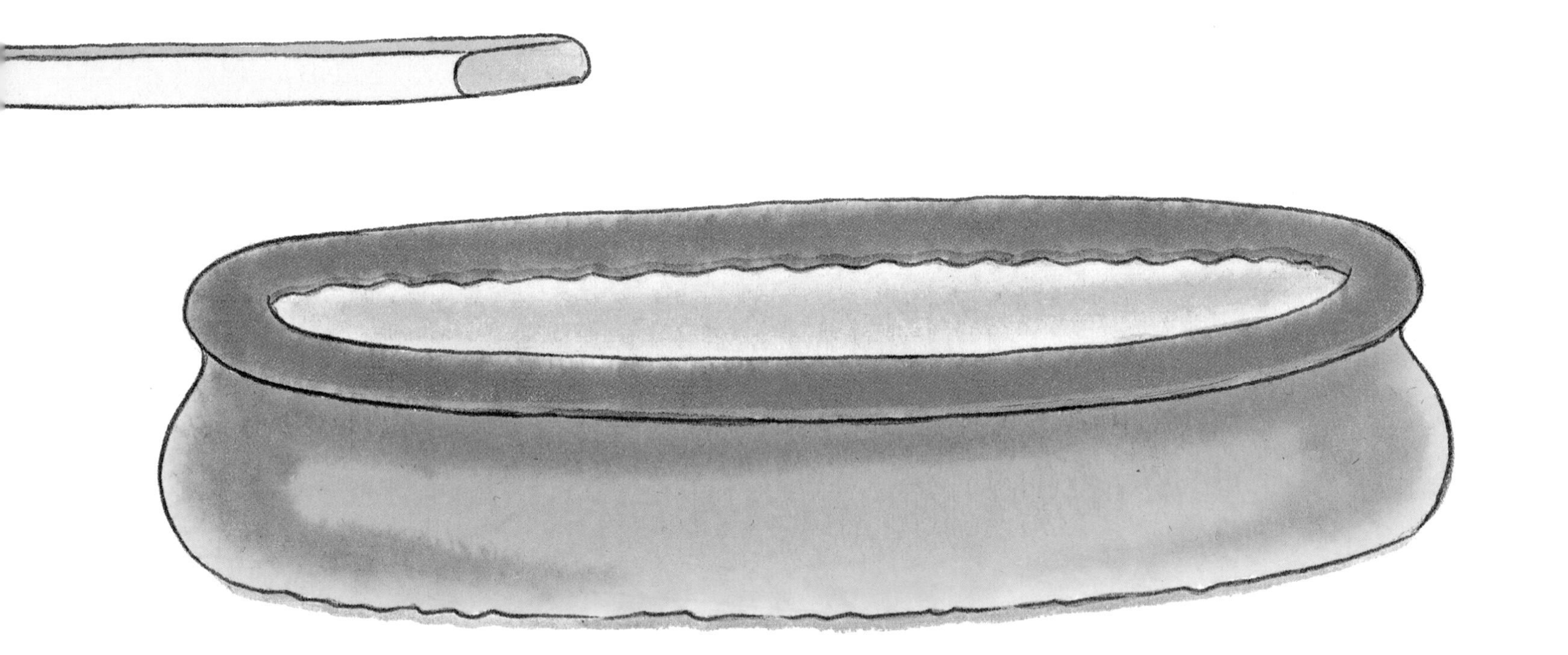

THREE fluffy ducks quack and flap and grin.

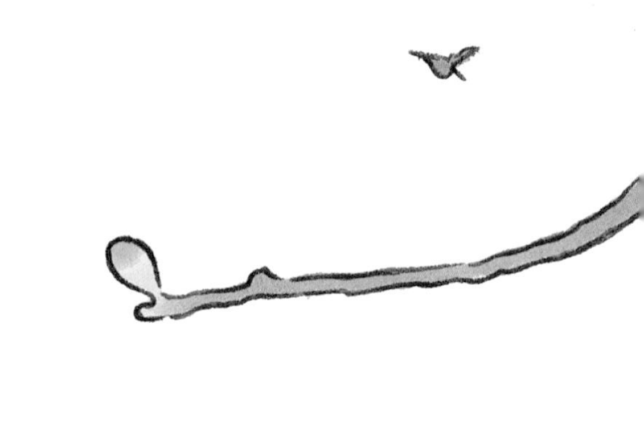

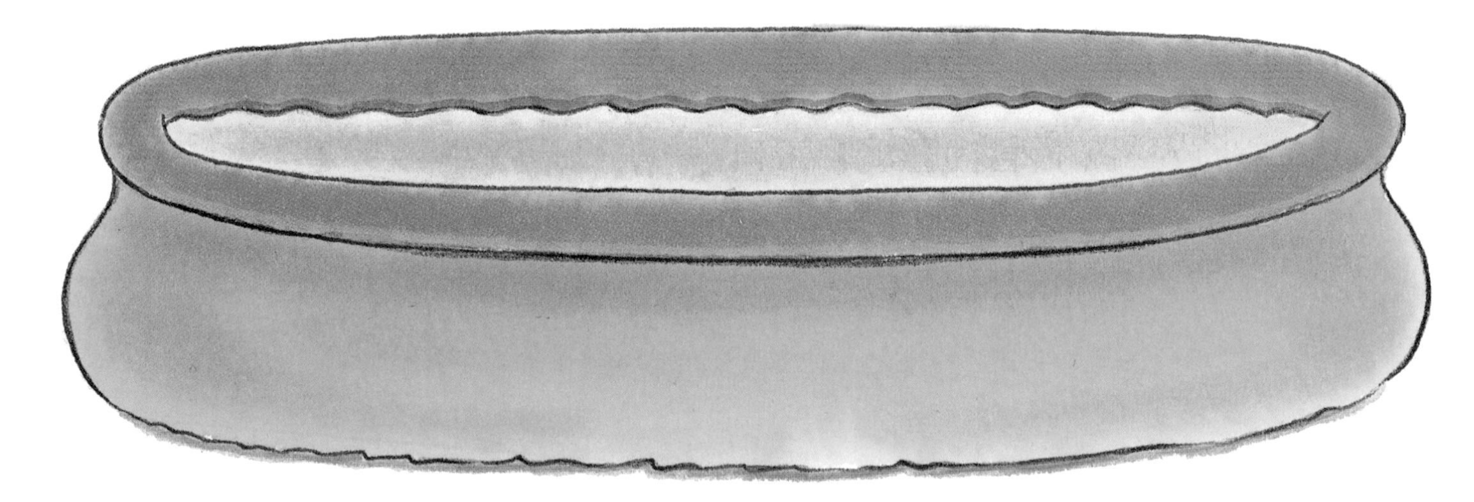

FOUR fluffy ducks say,

"Let's jump in!"

FIVE fluffy ducks – one gives the pool a try.

SIX fluffy ducks. Bounce.

B-doing.

Watch them fly!

SEVEN fluffy ducks. What a funny sight.

EIGHT fluffy ducks cry,

POP!
"Hold on tight!"

NINE fluffy ducks.
It's time they had a wash.

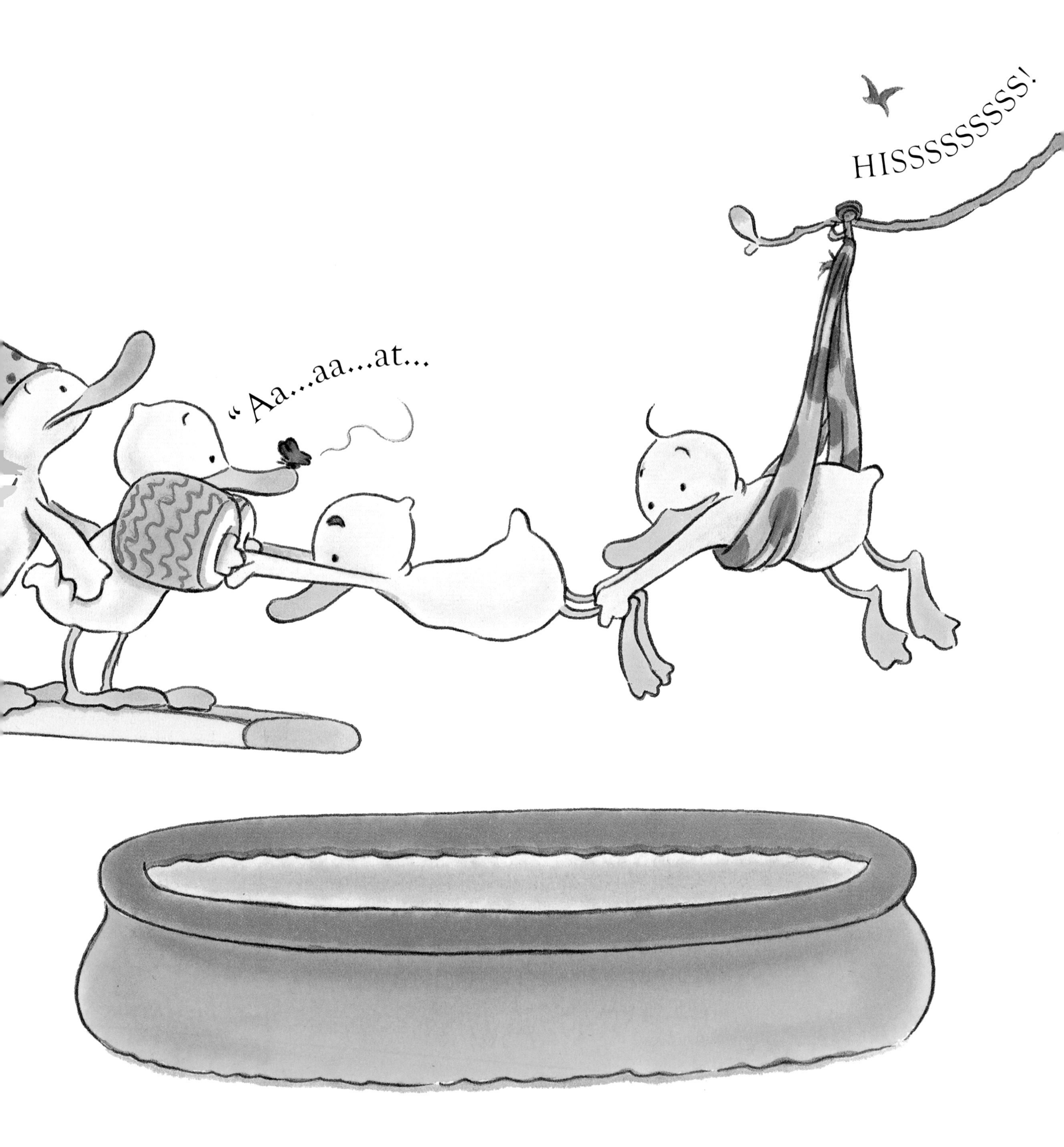
"Aa...aa...at...
HISSSSSSSSS!

...choo!"

TEN fluffy ducks...

...SPLISH, SPLASH,

SPLOSH!

Now let's count again...

1
2
3
4

6
7
8
9
10
5

7 8 4 3 6 2

9 2 6 9 7 5

5 7 5 8 9 3

1 10 2 1 4

8 4 5 3 2

5 7 9 4 5 10

LOOK OUT FOR THESE GREAT STORIES STARRING:

HUGLESS DOUGLAS

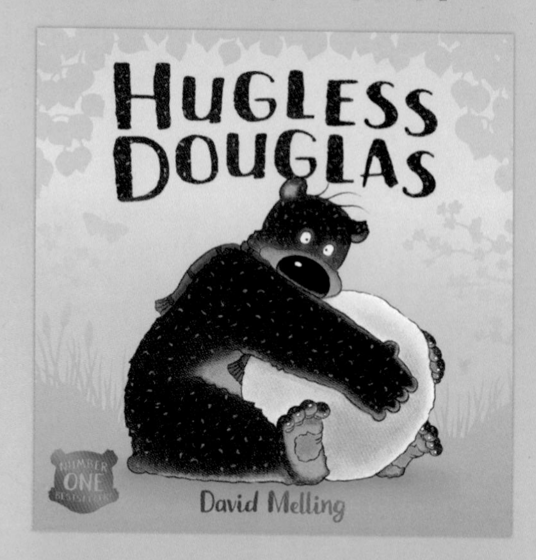
HUGLESS DOUGLAS
NUMBER ONE BESTSELLER
David Melling

DON'T WORRY, HUGLESS DOUGLAS
NUMBER ONE BESTSELLER
David Melling

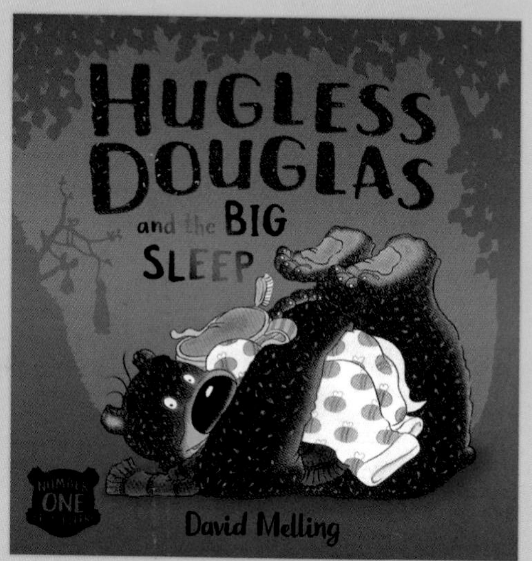
HUGLESS DOUGLAS and the BIG SLEEP
NUMBER ONE
David Melling

WE LOVE YOU, HUGLESS DOUGLAS
NUMBER ONE
David Melling

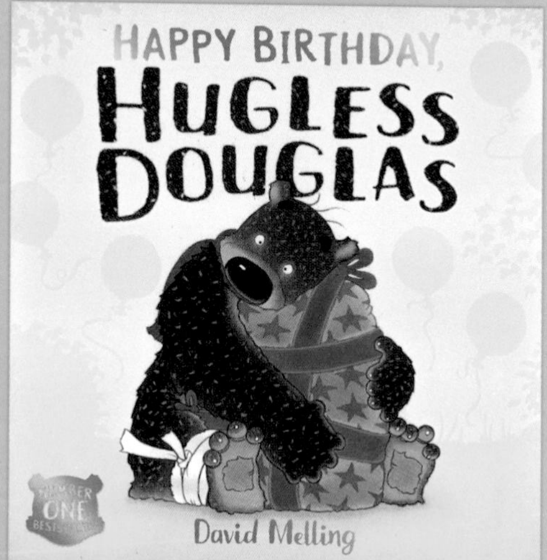
HAPPY BIRTHDAY, HUGLESS DOUGLAS
ONE
David Melling

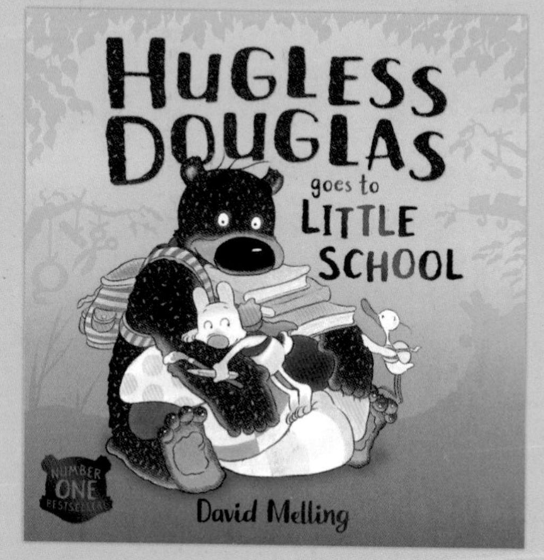
HUGLESS DOUGLAS goes to LITTLE SCHOOL
NUMBER ONE
David Melling

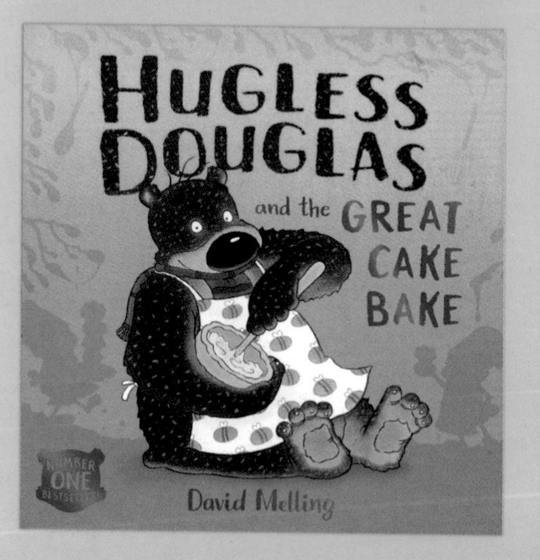
HUGLESS DOUGLAS and the GREAT CAKE BAKE
NUMBER ONE
David Melling